www.booksbyboxer.com

Bee Three Publishing is an imprint of Books By Boxer
Published by
Books By Boxer, Leeds, LS13 4BS, UK
Books by Boxer (EU), Dublin, D02 P593, IRELAND
Boxer Gifts LLC, 955 Sawtooth Oak Cir, VA 22802, USA
© Books By Boxer 2024
cs@boxer.gifts
All Rights Reserved
MADE IN CHINA
ISBN: 9781915410832

This book is produced from responsibly sourced paper to ensure forest management

YOU COMPLAIN THAT **THE YOUNGER GENERATION DON'T** **PLAY OUTSIDE** ANYMORE...

THEN COMPLAIN ABOUT THE NOISE WHEN THEY DO

YOU OFTEN SAY
'WHEN I WAS YOUR AGE
I OWNED A HOUSE,
WHAT'S YOUR EXCUSE?'...

YET YOU ARE FIRST TO COMPLAIN AT THE INCREASING COST OF EVERYDAY EXPENSES

YOU THINK THE YOUNGER GENERATION ARE FUSSY AND **ENTITLED...**

YET YOU ONLY USE A SPECIFIC BRAND OF TOILET ROLL

YOU HAVE A GLIMMER IN YOUR EYE...

CAUSED BY THE SUN
HITTING YOUR
BIFOCALS

YOUR KNEES
BUCKLE...

YOUR BELT WON'T....

YOU MAKE SURE TO **COMPLAIN** ABOUT THE WEATHER...

IN EVERY SEASON

YOU COMPLAIN ABOUT

EVERY

PARKED CAR IN THE LOT...

EXCEPT YOUR OWN

YOU HAVE A
FAVORITE
CHAIR...

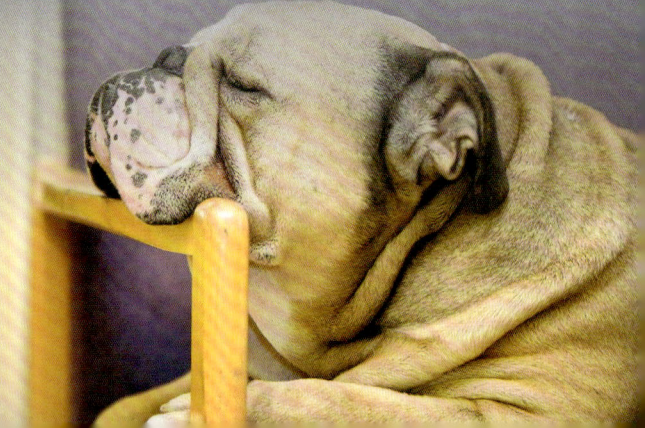

AND NOBODY ELSE IS ALLOWED TO USE IT

NOTHING CAN WAKE YOU UP FROM SLEEP

EXCEPT YOUR OWN SNORING!

YOUR IDEA OF A GOOD TIME...

IS A COMFY CHAIR
AND A QUIET
AFTERNOON

YOUR WORST FEAR IN LIFE...

IS BEING FORCED INTO SOCIAL PLANS

YOU NO LONGER RUN ERRANDS...

YOU WALK THEM... SLOWLY

YOUR SELECTIVE HEARING...

IS 100% DELIBERATE

YOU SHOW
YOUR ENTHUSIASM...

WITH AN EYE ROLL AND A SIGH

YOU HAVE A **LONG LIST** OF EXCUSES...

TO AVOID MAKING PLANS

YOU STOP MAKING **EXCUSES** TO LEAVE EARLY...

BY NEVER TURNING UP IN THE FIRST PLACE

COUPLES IN
IN MATCHING
OUTFITS...

MAKE
YOU WINCE

YOU COMPLAIN ABOUT MODERN FASHION...

AND THE LACK OF GOOD POCKETS

YOU REFUSE TO USE A SATNAV...

THEN DRIVE AROUND IN CIRCLES

YOU CARRY A BACK-UP PAIR OF GLASSES

FOR YOUR BACK-UP PAIR OF GLASSES

YOU HAVE **THREE** CONVERSATION MODES...

THE WEATHER, THE YOUTH, THE PRICE OF POTATOES

YOU HAVE STRONG OPINIONS ABOUT...

YOUR NEIGHBORHOOD
BIN COLLECTION
DAYS

"NO TALKING BEFORE COFFEE"

YOUR FOOD BEING TOO SPICY...

CAN RUIN YOUR ENTIRE DAY

YOU COMPLAIN ABOUT PEOPLE NOT WEARING PROPER FOOTWEAR...

YET YOU SPEND EVERY WAKING HOUR IN SOCKS AND SANDALS

YOU GET **MAD** THAT YOU'RE LEFT OUT OF SOCIAL GATHERINGS...

BUT WOULDN'T HAVE GONE ANYWAY

YOU HATE WHEN PEOPLE CUT QUEUES...

YET CUT
IN THE QUEUE
YOURSELF

YOU ORDER YOUR FOOD SHOP ONLINE...

SO YOU DON'T HAVE TO INTERACT WITH OTHERS

YOU **COMPLAIN** ABOUT CARS PLAYING **LOUD** MUSIC...

YET LISTEN TO THE
NEWS & SPORTS
RADIO ON
FULL VOLUME

YOU PRETEND TO BE OUT...

TO AVOID UNEXPECTED GUESTS

YOU GET
ROAD RAGE...

WHEN USING A SHOPPING CART

A CAR FORGETTING TO INDICATE...

CAN SEND YOU INTO A WILD RANT

YOU TURN YOUR LIGHTS OUT...

TO DETER
TRICK-OR-TREATERS

YOU COMPLAIN ABOUT SOCIAL MEDIA....

BUT SPEND ALL DAY SHARING FACEBOOK POSTS

NOBODY AROUND YOU IS ALLOWED TO COMPLAIN...

UNTIL THEY GET TO YOUR AGE

BEING **STUCK** BEHIND SOMEONE WALKING SLOW...

FILLS YOU WITH RAGE

IF A STORE IS
CARD ONLY...

YOU'LL TAKE YOUR BUSINESS ELSEWHERE

YOU SAY 'KIDS THESE DAYS AND THEIR PHONES'...

BUT WATCH FACEBOOK VIDEOS AT FULL VOUME IN PUBLIC

YOU'RE ONLY
GRUMBLING...

WHEN YOU'RE AWAKE

YOU HAVE A
PET HATE FOR...

CARS WITH
HIGH BEAMS

YOU **HIDE** DOWN GROCERY STORE AISLES...

TO AVOID TALKING TO PEOPLE YOU KNOW

YOUR FRONT DOOR ONLY OPENS...

FOR THE DELIVERY MAN

THE ONLY TIKTOK YOU KNOW...

IS THE ONE THAT COMES FROM A CLOCK

YOU KNOW WHAT FOOD YOU LIKE...

AND DON'T CARE TO TRY ANYTHING NEW

THE ONLY PLANS YOU LIKE...

ARE THE ONES THAT DON'T EXIST

YOU HAVE YOUR OWN SPECIAL MUG...

WHICH NOBODY ELSE IS ALLOWED TO USE

THE ONE THING YOU'LL NEVER UNDERSTAND...

IS ALL
THESE NEW
HAIRSTYLES

THE WORLD ISN'T GETTING MORE ANNOYING, YOU'RE JUST GETTING GRUMPIER!